Brown Bear and Wilbur Wolf

Written by Sarah Parry

Illustrated by Judy Musselle

Collins

Brown Bear was hungry. He'd been asleep all winter.
He came out of his den and stretched. The snow had
melted and the grass was green. Brown Bear looked around
him and sniffed the air, but he couldn't smell anything.

3

He went into the forest to look for berries, but he couldn't smell anything.

He went to the river to look for fish, but he couldn't smell anything.

"I've lost my smell," he said sadly to himself. "How will I find any food?" He lay down in a meadow by the river and tried to remember all his favourite smells – the smell of trees, the smell of new grass, the smell of apples and leaves, of berries, of rain and snow.

"I feel so lonely without my smell," Brown Bear said.
"Perhaps it wouldn't be so bad if I had a friend to talk to."
But he was all alone.

The birds thought Brown Bear looked sad, so they flew
down to play with him.

Brown Bear was pleased to see them and jumped up, but
the birds got a fright and flew away.

The beaver saw Brown Bear in the field and thought he looked sad. He called Brown Bear over to his dam.

Brown Bear ran towards him, but the beaver
got a fright and hid under the branches.

The deer walked into the field and saw Brown Bear looking sad, so they skipped towards him.

Brown Bear stood on his back legs to say hello,
but the deer got a fright and turned back.

Brown Bear lay down. He was all alone and was still hungry.

Wilbur Wolf came out of the forest. He was old and tired and had been looking for food all winter. He saw Brown Bear in the field and walked slowly towards him. "Maybe Brown Bear can tell me where to find some food," Wilbur said to himself.

Brown Bear was too tired and hungry to get up when Wilbur came near, so Wilbur wasn't scared. They lay in the tall grass, and Brown Bear explained that he'd lost his smell.

"Without my smell, how will I find any food?"
Brown Bear asked.

Wilbur shrugged, "I'm old and weak," he said.
"How will I catch any food?"

They lay quietly for a while and then Brown Bear said, "Perhaps we can look for food together. You can be my smell and I'm strong enough to catch food for us both."

19

"We can try," Wilbur said. And they did. From that day they stayed together – Wilbur would sniff out the berries or the fish and strong Brown Bear would gather enough food for them to share.

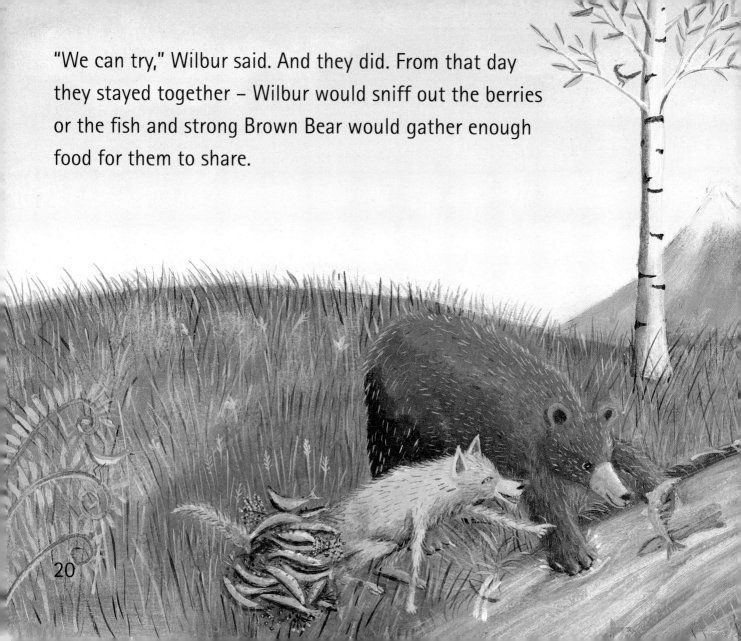

So they walked the valleys and mountains,
forests and riverbeds together and neither
ever felt lonely or hungry again.

Looking for a friend

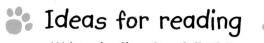

Ideas for reading

Written by Clare Dowdall, PhD
Lecturer and Primary Literacy Consultant

Reading objectives:
- draw on what they already know
- read words containing taught GPCs, –ing and –ed
- predict what might happen on the basis of what has been read so far
- make inferences on the basis of what is being said and done
- participate in discussion about what is read to them, taking turns and listening to what others say

Spoken language objectives:
- participate in discussions
- select and use appropriate registers for effective communication
- participate in discussions and presentations

Curriculum links: Citizenship; Science

Resources: whiteboard

Interest words: lonely, stretched, sniffed, favourite, fright, skipped

Word count: 414

Build a context for reading

- Ask children what their favourite smells are and why. Discuss why it is important to have a sense of smell. Ask children what animals might use their sense of smell for, e.g. dogs and cats for sniffing their food and checking that it is good.

- Show children the front cover. Read the title and ask the children to suggest some facts about wolves and bears and their habitats. List the facts on a whiteboard.

- Read the blurb together and focus on the word *hibernating*. Remind children of some strategies for tackling longer unfamiliar words, e.g. using phonic strategies, looking for units of meaning, breaking the word into syllables before blending. Check that children understand what the term means.

Understand and apply reading strategies

- Read p2 together, aloud. Ask children to find words that describe what Brown Bear did when he awoke, e.g. stretched, looked, sniffed. Help children to notice that these words have *ed* endings.

- Ask children to read to p7 aloud. What sort of voice do they think Brown Bear would have? Model reading the speech with a sad voice. Ask children to predict what Wilbur Wolf might do to help him.